RADIO ASTRONOMY

RADIO ASTRONOMY

ALAN E. NOURSE

Franklin Watts
New York/London/Toronto
Sydney/1989
A Venture Book

Illustrations by: Vantage Art

Photographs courtesy of:
Bell Labs: p. 10; NRAO/AUI: pp. 14, 50, 52, 74
(both); California Institute of Technology: p.
16; Yerkes Observatory: pp. 20 (top), 43, 57,
59; British Library, London: p. 20 (bottom);
Bettmann Archives: pp. 21, 22, 24, 25, 30, 32,
33, 81; UPI/Bettmann Newsphotos: pp. 41, 45,
48; National Optical Astronomy Observatories:
p. 70; Photo Researchers: p. 83 (Ronald Royer/
Science Photo Library).

Library of Congress Cataloging-in-Publication Data

Nourse, Alan Edward.
Radio Astronomy / by Alan E. Nourse.
p.   cm.—(A Venture book)
Bibliography: p.
Includes index.
Summary: Describes radio astronomy and how it
helps scientists study the universe.
ISBN 0-531-10811-2
1. Radio astronomy—Juvenile literature.
[1. Radio astronomy.]
I. Title.
QB4789.N68   1989
522'.682—dc20   89-32405   CIP   AC

CONTENTS

RADIO ASTRONOMY

1

WHISPERS
FROM THE SKY

One day in 1931—more than fifty-five years ago—a twenty-six-year-old American scientist made a discovery so seemingly simple, yet so astounding, that it was destined to revolutionize the whole science of astronomy, the study of the planets, stars, and galaxies.

Strangely enough, this young man wasn't an astronomer at all. Karl Jansky was a radio engineer. In those days the science of transmitting human voices by radio waves was in its infancy. Jansky was employed by the Bell Telephone Laboratories to try to solve a constant, annoying problem with long-distance radio transmissions such as ship-to-shore telephone messages—the loud bursts of noisy static that constantly interfered with reception. This crackling "radio noise" seemed to arise from many sources—thunderstorms, passing airplanes, nearby electrical equipment, and so forth.

As he studied this radio interference, however, Jansky noticed something odd that nobody had ever reported before. Aside from the bursts of loud, crackling static interfering with his telephones, there seemed to be another kind of "radio noise" going on—a quiet, constant "background static" from some source he couldn't identify. It seemed to be coming from the sky, with its direction moving steadily from day to day! At first Jansky thought the Sun must be to blame, but this signal source seemed to be crossing the sky a little faster than the Sun moved each day. Finally Jansky decided that these "whispers from the sky" had to

Historical photograph of Karl Jansky and the rotating antenna with which he discovered radio waves in space

be coming from somewhere far outside our solar system, out toward the constellation Sagittarius, the direction of the very center of our Milky Way galaxy. This was an area that astronomers had never been able to observe very well because vast clouds of interstellar gas and dust blocked their view. But radio signals seemed to be coming through perfectly well.

Karl Jansky didn't really understand what it was that he had discovered. He wasn't even terribly interested—it didn't help him solve *his* problem with radio static. But like any good scientist who notices something odd going on, he reported his findings. Oddly enough, most of the prominent astronomers of the day weren't much interested in these "whispers from the sky," either. Nobody at that time realized that Jansky, without knowing it, had become the father of a whole new science to be known as *radio astronomy*. It remained for a single enthusiastic amateur astronomer to nurse that baby science to life single-handedly.

AN AMATEUR TAKES OVER

Even in his teens, Grote Reber was deeply interested in amateur radio communication. As a student at the Illinois Institute of Technology, he heard about Jansky's "whispers from the sky" and set out to study them on his own. Of course he realized that these were not intelligent signals from other planets—they had to be some kind of random radio signals generated by violent atomic or electronic storms going on in the vicinity of distant stars. But here on Earth they were very faint. Some way was needed to gather and receive them so that the sources could be pinpointed and charted.

In 1937, in his own backyard, Reber spent his own time and money building an instrument intended to do just that. One part of the instrument was a "dish" or reflector, 32 feet (9.8 m) in diameter, built in the slightly oval shape called a *parabola* (Figure 1). This particular curve could "catch" radio waves coming in from space and reflect them to a single point of *focus* out in front of the dish. At this focal point Reber placed a receiving antenna—really just a kind of radio antenna—that would pick up the focused and concentrated radio waves. The radio signals from the sky were then conducted to an amplifier (to make them louder) and recorded on a graph on a revolving drum. Grote Reber had, in fact, built the world's first radio telescope in his own backyard.

THE ONLY
RADIO ASTRONOMER
IN THE WORLD

He used it, too. Indeed, for several years he was literally the one and only radio astronomer in the world. Of course, what he had built was totally different from any previous telescope. To a nonastronomer it might have seemed a rather stupid instrument—and mysterious as well.

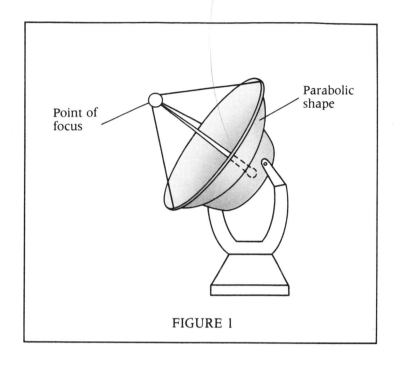

Point of focus

Parabolic shape

FIGURE 1

Reber's telescope consisted of a dish with a parabolic surface, which could reflect radio waves collected from space to a single point of focus in front of the dish. The larger the dish, the more radio waves are collected, producing a clearer, brighter image of the source.

Unlike the familiar light-gathering telescopes, a radio telescope does not produce a visible picture. You can't "look through" a radio telescope and see anything. The "images" it produces are recorded in the form of graphs, charts, magnetic recording

tapes, or computer data. You can't hear anything, either. The scratchy "radio noise" associated with a radio telescope is not actually sound from space; it comes from the receiving equipment.

Reber knew all this, of course. He simply wanted to use his radio telescope to locate and map where these signals came from in the sky. He soon found that they did not come from just one area alone. There were many "hot spots" in the sky emitting radio waves stronger than the background whispering. One source—surprisingly weak—was our Sun itself. One source was in the constellation Cygnus, another in Cassiopeia. Yet another source was the Crab Nebula, the expanding cloud of gas and dust that remained from a supernova explosion (a colossal star explosion) known from history to have been first seen in the year 1054. (The explosion itself must have occurred some six thousand years earlier; it simply took the light from that explosion that long to reach us.)

Reber called these sources "radio stars" whether they were actually stars or not. (Today they are usually called "radio sources.") Some of his radio stars matched up with known, visible

An electrical engineer, Grote Reber, built the first radio telescope designed for astronomical observation. It took him four months to build at a cost of $4,000.

stars, but many of them didn't. Nor were they all concentrated in our own Milky Way galaxy. At least one of Reber's radio stars later turned out to be a distant pair of galaxies colliding with each other. By the time Reber began reporting his findings in 1942, it was clear that his crude radio telescope made it possible to identify and map objects and events in the sky that *couldn't be seen at all* with ordinary light-gathering telescopes.

In short, the newborn science of radio astronomy provided a completely new way of observing and studying the universe around us. In the brief span of less than fifty years, astronomers using radio telescopes have made astounding discoveries about the shape, nature, and history of the universe.

The Crab Nebula, whose stellar debris left over from the catastrophic death of a star appears as an intense source of radio radiation

2

WINDOWS TO
THE UNIVERSE

Many scientists studying the world around them take specimens into the laboratory to examine them closely. It's different with astronomers. The "specimens" they study—the planets, stars, and galaxies—are far too distant to be examined directly. Astronomers have always had to observe the heavens by *indirectly* studying and analyzing messages from heavenly objects that have come to Earth from afar. And until the 1940s these messages had always been in the form of *visible light waves.*

THE ANCIENT
ASTRONOMERS

Astronomy is one of the oldest of all the sciences. Astronomers have been studying the heavens for more than five thousand years. By naked-eye observation they learned that the

Opposite: A miniature showing Arabian astronomers at work. Above top: The zodiacal constellations as depicted in A Compilation of Leopold of Austria *(1520) and (bottom) an astronomical table recording the rising points of the constellations from a Moslem manuscript.*

stars are different from one another. Some are blue, some red, and some white. Some are very bright, others much dimmer. The ancient astronomers also discovered two very different *kinds* of "stars." Although most stars seemed fixed in the same place in the sky compared to the others, year after year, a few "wanderers" moved around from one place to another. We now know that those "wanderers" are the planets of our Solar System.

Of course, everything those ancient astronomers could learn about the stars and planets came from the light they could see with the naked eye. For example, almost anyone could see Mizar, the

Arabian astronomers, in a woodcut dating back to 1513, are shown recording their observations.

bright star second from the end of the handle of the Big Dipper, but only those with keen eyes could see Alcor, Mizar's dim companion star. It is said that the ancient Arabs used this as a kind of vision test! (See if you can see Alcor on a clear summer night.) In fact, the ancient astronomers learned an amazing amount about the heavens with naked-eye observation alone, but without a "better way to see" they were forever limited.

GALILEO
AND THE TELESCOPE

Astronomy's dependence on naked-eye observation ended in the year 1609, when the Italian scientist Galileo heard about a "magnifying tube" with glass lenses just invented in Holland. Within a few months Galileo had built his own, with a magnifying power of three times, and he began searching the sky with the instrument—the first effective *telescope*. A later model of his magnified thirty-two times.

Galileo made many observations and discoveries with his new telescope. He could actually see mountains on the Moon. He observed sunspots on the Sun, and by tracking them day by day, proved that the Sun turned on its own axis once every twenty-seven days. He found that the stars always appeared as pinpoints of light, while the planets appeared as small disks, thus proving they were much closer to earth than the stars were. And he discovered the four major moons of Jupiter, invis-

Galileo (1564–1642) demonstrates his telescope to the Senate of Venice.

ible to the naked eye, and proved that they moved in orbit around the giant planet. (You can see them yourself with a powerful pair of binoculars or a small telescope.)

As great a scientist as he was, Galileo was not always right. When he tried to measure the speed of light—a matter of great importance to modern astronomers, as we will see—he failed completely. Galileo was convinced that light, like any other

Galileo's telescope on exhibit in Florence, Italy.

kind of signal, must travel from one point to another at a given, measurable speed. His goal was to measure the time it took a light beam to travel from one hilltop to another, and then, knowing the distance between hilltops, to calculate the speed of the light beam. His plan was very simple. On a dark, moonless night, with an assistant watching from a distant hilltop, Galileo would unmask his lantern. The instant his assistant saw the light, he would unmask his lantern in turn. The difference in time between opening the first lantern and observing the answering light from the second should then be equivalent to the time required for the light beam to travel to the distant hilltop and back again.

It was a neat, well-thought-out experiment, but it just didn't work. Galileo saw the answering light from the distant hilltop appear the very same instant that he opened his own lantern. There was no time lag, and the same thing happened no matter how many times he tried it. Galileo's conclusion was that light had *no* measurable speed, but spread instantly to all parts of the universe. Today, of course, we know that that conclusion was wrong—light does travel at a measurable speed, but that speed is exceedingly high. Light travels 186,300 miles (299,800 km) in a single second. There was nothing wrong with Galileo's experiment; he simply had no way to measure that incredible swift speed over the short distance from one hilltop to another.

Galileo failed to measure the speed of light, but he *did* spread the word far and wide about his telescopic observations. Soon bigger and better telescopes were being built and used. Two main kinds of telescopes were devised. The first, like Galileo's, had glass lenses in either end of a long tube. The large lens in one end gathered light from the stars and bent or *refracted* it down the length of the tube to focus on a smaller magnifying eyepiece, or *ocular*, lens. This was a so-called *refractor telescope* (Figure 2). But astronomers soon found that the bigger they made their light-gathering lenses, the more fuzzy the image became, surrounded by rainbowlike halos (we will see why a bit later). A different kind of telescope, the so-called *reflector telescope*, solved this problem. Here a curved reflecting mirror, ground in the slightly oval shape of a parabola, was placed in the bottom end of an empty tube. Light from the stars was gathered by this mirror and reflected to a focus on an objective lens suspended at the mirror's focal point (Figure 3). The result was a clear, crisp image.

Reflector telescopes could be made much larger than refractor telescopes, and thus more powerful in terms of light-gathering ability. In fact, the size and power of a reflector telescope is limited only by the size of mirror you can make. The Hale telescope on Mount Palomar, with its 200-inch (508-cm) reflecting mirror, is the biggest such telescope in the United States and is considered the finest in the world. There is also a 236-inch (600-cm) reflector telescope in the Soviet Union. Any single-mirror telescope much bigger than this is impractical because the mirror is too difficult to manufacture and too big and heavy to handle. But

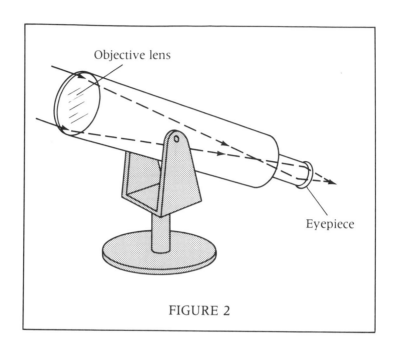

Objective lens

Eyepiece

FIGURE 2

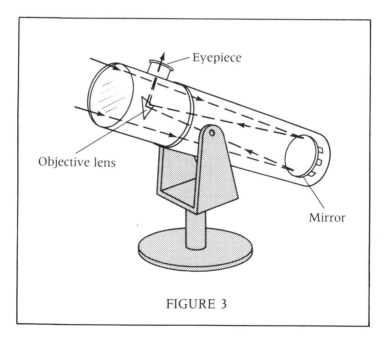

Eyepiece

Objective lens

Mirror

FIGURE 3

astronomers today are getting around this problem by building much larger, multi-mirror reflecting telescopes.

Although light-receiving telescopes have greatly enlarged our understanding of our Sun and Solar System, our Milky Way galaxy, and the universe of galaxies beyond it, they are limited to observing messages coming to us in the form of light from the stars and galaxies. Nobody originally suspected that there might be invisible messages that could tell us far more.

THE ELECTROMAGNETIC SPECTRUM

Until the late 1600s everyone had always assumed that light was simply light—a form of energy we could perceive because our eyes were made to respond to it. Then in 1666 the great English scientist and mathematician Isaac Newton

Top: A refractor *telescope. The large glass lens on the end gathers light from the stars and refracts it down the length of the tube to focus on a smaller, magnifying eyepiece. Bottom: A* reflector *telescope. A curved reflecting mirror at the bottom end of the tube gathers light from the stars and reflects it to a focus on an objective lens suspended at the mirror's focal point.*

The Palomar Observatory's 200-inch telescope near San Diego, California, was the brainchild of Dr. George Ellery Hale. The entire telescope weighs in excess of 500 tons and the mirror, which weighs 14¾ tons, took eleven years to build.

discovered that light was not so "simple" after all. He found that a beam of sunlight, passed through a triangular *prism*—a triangular block of glass or quartz—would be broken up into a whole rainbow band, or *spectrum* of different colors: red, orange, yellow, green, blue, indigo and violet. The white sunlight beam was bent, or *refracted*, in passing through the prism, but each component color was bent slightly more than the last because each color had its own slightly different characteristic *wavelength*—violet the shortest, red the longest.

This was why large telescopes of Galileo's type produced such fuzzy, rainbow-ringed images. Light from the stars was broken up into its various colors as it passed through the telescope lens, just as through a prism, and it was that broken-up light that reached the magnifying lens at the lower end of the telescope. The mirror of a reflecting telescope did away with this problem because it reflected all wavelengths of light to the same focal point.

Newton's spectrum of colored light (Figure 4) of different wavelengths was a breakthrough. But there seemed to be more to this spectrum than just visible light of different colors. For example, most of the heat in sunlight seemed to be concentrated in a band of invisible "light" or energy located just below the band of visible red light, where it faded into blackness—a band of "infrared" light. And just above the point where the violet band of visible light faded into blackness was a band of invisible "ultraviolet" light—a wavelength of light or energy that you can't see, and which isn't hot,

The English physicist and mathematician, Sir Isaac Newton (1642–1727), analyzes a ray of sunlight in this engraving by Loudan.

Isaac Newton guides a beam of light through a triangular prism. The experiment enabled him to discover the inherent properties of light.

but which can give you a nasty sunburn, or make many substances (including your teeth) glow in the dark.

As if this discovery of "light that you can't see" wasn't enough, scientists soon took it one step further. They found that there was a whole variety of different invisible waves detectable on either side of visible colored light on this energy spectrum. Whenever atomic particles get bounced

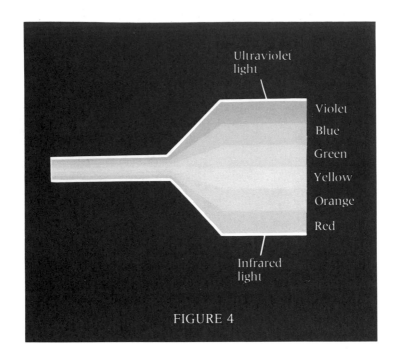

Ultraviolet light

Violet
Blue
Green
Yellow
Orange
Red

Infrared light

FIGURE 4

Invisible bands of ''infrared'' and ''ultraviolet'' light can be found at each end of Newton's spectrum of visible colored light.

about violently—in an X-ray tube, for example, or on the surface or interiors of stars, or in turbulent clouds of interstellar gas—they emit energy in the form of a wide variety of invisible waves in addition to visible light waves. All those waves, whether invisible or visible, travel through space at the speed of light. Only a very small part of this spectrum of waves is made up of visible light waves, which have extremely short wavelengths, ranging from 7/100,000 of a centimeter for red light to 4/100,000 of a centimeter for violet light— shorter than the length of many bacteria. We are immediately aware of light waves because our eyes *see* different wavelengths of visible light as different colors. Invisible waves with longer wavelengths than red light include *infrared waves, microwaves* (the same high-energy waves that cook your food in a microwave oven), the longer microwaves that are bounced off distant objects for *radar* detection, and the still longer *radio waves* we use to transmit television signals and FM and AM radio signals. Invisible waves with shorter wavelengths than violet light in the spectrum include *X rays, gamma rays,* and the *cosmic rays* that constantly bombard us from outer space. All of these waves, we now know, are forms of energy that are flung out when atomic particles are agitated in violent collisions such as those that occur constantly on the surfaces of stars or among gas clouds in space.

Scientists now speak of this whole band of waves, including light waves, as the *electromagnetic spectrum.* You can see it diagramed in Figure 5. Astronomers using conventional light-gathering telescopes have always been limited to what they could observe with the light-wave portion of the spectrum. But radio astronomy works with the different waves that lie on either side of light waves in that spectrum—waves that were completely invisible until radio telescopes were invented. (Of

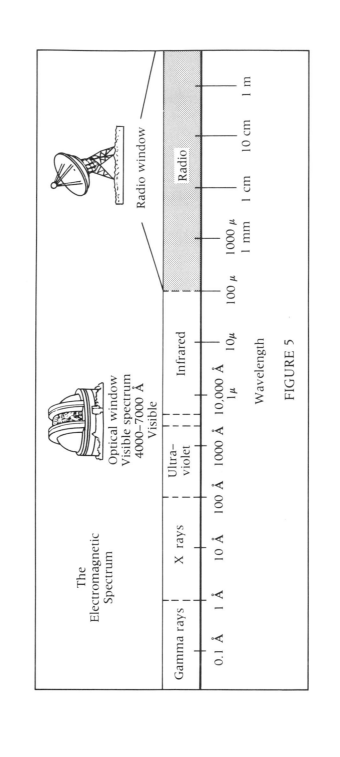

FIGURE 5

course, they are still invisible, but can be gathered, observed, and analyzed indirectly with radio telescopes.) With Grote Reber's first radio telescope, the science of radio astronomy began, and a whole new generation of telescopes was invented to receive and study these invisible waves.

The electromagnetic spectrum encompasses not only white light but a whole variety of invisible waves of varying wavelengths.

3

RADIO
TELESCOPES

It was in 1937 that Grote Reber built the first crude radio telescope and began mapping a variety of "radio objects" in the sky, some also visible to conventional light-gathering telescopes, some not. But the great surge of interest in radio astronomy did not really begin until the end of World War II in 1945.

Why did it take so long? For one thing, the techniques for receiving, manipulating, and analyzing radio waves were still in their infancy before the war. Many of these techniques, including the use of radar, were not worked out or fine-tuned until the war years, so radio telescopes didn't become practical as scientific instruments until the late 1940s and early 1950s.

One of the early pioneers in radio astronomy was an Englishman named Bernard Lovell, working at Manchester University in England. Lovell was naturally drawn to radio astronomy. Early in his career he had studied cosmic rays—high-energy atomic particles constantly bombarding the Earth from far out in space. Then during the war he was involved in radar research. So by the early 1950s he was able to get a major radio telescope built at Jodrell Bank near Manchester. Later he was knighted in recognition of his work.

Lovell's radio telescope was a major achievement. There had been nothing basically wrong with Reber's pioneering radio telescope, but it was very limited. Its receiving dish was only 32 feet (9.8 m) across, so its reception was limited and it was clumsy to handle and "aim." By comparison, Lovell's radio telescope at Jodrell Bank, which took six years to build, was a model of sophistication. Its receiving dish was 250 feet (76 m) across. Massively mounted with parts from revolving battleship turrets, this giant dish was fully steerable, so that it could be turned to face any portion of the sky at will—or moved to follow a heavenly object. One of its first uses, just as construction was completed, was to track *Sputnik I*, the first man-made Earth satellite, launched into orbit by the Soviets in 1957. Since then this telescope has become one of the most useful instruments on earth for tracking orbiting satellites.

Basically, Lovell's radio telescope worked like Reber's. Silent, invisible radio signals from space were gathered by the receiving dish and reflected to focus on a receiving antenna suspended at the focal point in front of the dish. From there the signals were carried to various kinds of recording

This radio telescope (right) at Jodrell Bank in Cheshire, England, has been tracking satellites since 1957. A newer radio telescope (left) has a 125-foot movable dish, about half the size of the original.

equipment and the data recorded on graphs, charts, magnetic tapes, etc.

Even today virtually all radio telescopes work in this general way. The Jodrell Bank telescope could be used not only for receiving radio signals from heavenly objects, but for transmitting signals as well. One of its earliest uses was to send out radar signals to bounce off distant objects and then receive and analyze those signals as they were reflected back. Much has been learned about the nature of comets, for example, by bouncing radar signals off their tails—those vast sweeps of ice particles, dust, and gas that form as a comet approaches the Sun. Radar signals bounced off the surface of Venus have revealed many details of the surface of that planet—towering mountains and vast plains—forever hidden from view by that planet's perpetual cloud cover. And radar-telescope techniques made it possible to map surface elevations on the Moon plus or minus a few inches, and thereby provided vital information when the American moon landings were planned. The surface of Mars has also been mapped, and new information about the nature of Jupiter and Saturn was also gained before the Pioneer satellites went out for direct exploration.

THE ARECIBO
RADIO TELESCOPE

Fine as the Jodrell Bank radio telescope was, it still had the limitation of *base*—

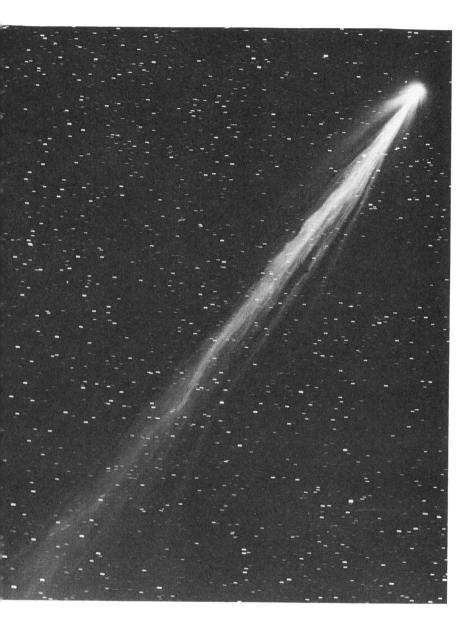

*A comet streaks across the sky, showing
a tail made up of many streamers*

the width of its receiving dish—and *resolution*—the ability to achieve razor-sharp radio images of very distant heavenly bodies within and outside our Milky Way galaxy. The same problems arose with radio telescopes built at the Cavendish Laboratories in Britain and at the University of Sydney in Australia. The way around this problem, of course, was to build a telescope with a larger "base," that is, a wider span for the receiving dish.

There were two ways this could be done. One was to build a single-unit radio telescope with an enormously huge receiving dish. This was exactly what was done near the town of Arecibo on the north coast of Puerto Rico. Completed in the spring of 1963, the Arecibo radio telescope is one of the most remarkable astronomical instruments ever devised, and one of the modern Wonders of the World as well. Built by the United States government and operated jointly by the National Aeronautics and Space Administration (NASA) and Cornell University, this enormous radio-radar telescope has for its reflecting dish a huge cup of wire mesh 1,000 feet (305 m) in diameter, built (from chicken wire, of all things!) into a natural valley in the Puerto Rican jungle. The wire is "plated" with perforated aluminum strips, and breaks in the dish are repaired by workmen walking down to the damage area on water skis. High over the dish (dangling fifty stories in the air) is the receiving and transmitting equipment of the telescope, installed on a cradle of steel girders weighing 600 tons and suspended in the air by huge

Nestled in the hills of Puerto Rico, the Arecibo telescope is one of the largest in the world. It beams radar signals at the planet Venus, and whatever bounces back to Arecibo may be able to produce the best map ever made of Venus.

cables supported by three concrete towers rising from the edges of the dish. A built-in laser "eye" can confirm, amazingly enough, that the entire curvature of the dish at any given time is perfect to a tolerance (or variance) of 1/8 of an inch (0.32 cm) or less.

Of course, this enormous dish is not steerable, but a limited amount of "aiming" is possible by moving the receiving and transmitting unit on its cradle in the air. The telescope is both a radio telescope (equipped to receive radio waves from deep space) and a radar telescope (able to transmit signals outward). At full transmission, the Arecibo telescope can send out a signal so powerful that to a similar "radio eye" located in a far distant star system, it would seem ten billion times more "radio bright" than our own Sun.

It was this powerful signal-transmission capability that led to one of the Arecibo telescope's most fascinating projects: the Search for Extraterrestrial Intelligence project, known as SETI. Many scientists believe that we are not alone in the universe, that among all the billions of different stars there are surely some, like our own, that have formed planets on which life has evolved and intelligence appeared. But how to contact such intelligence? Astronomers like Carl Sagan of Cornell University argue that if we could receive naturally generated radio signals from distant stars, then intelligent creatures with radio telescopes on planets of distant stars should be able to receive man-made signals beamed from Earth. If the signals were fashioned correctly and transmitted in some orderly, repetitive way, an intelligent creature receiving them on a distant world would recognize that they had to be coming from another intelligent race—and might send a similar signal back.

In the mid-1970s, the Arecibo telescope began beaming just such a code signal of radio frequencies toward the heavens. Astronomers estimate that it ought to reach some two hundred nearby stars (by "nearby" we mean stars located within 15 or 20 light-years away). No response has been detected yet, but that's hardly surprising. Since radio signals travel through space at the speed of light, it would take twenty years for a radio signal just to reach a star 20 light-years away, and another twenty years for a return signal to reach Earth. Although a similar, earlier attempt in the 1960s, known as Project Ozma, had been given up as a lost cause, the Arecibo SETI project used equipment a dozen times more powerful and sensitive. It is far too early yet to write it off as a failure.

LARGE-ARRAY
TELESCOPES

Once the Arecibo telescope was built, it seemed impractical to try to achieve more accuracy and resolution in a radio telescope by building a still bigger receiving dish. Instead, astronomers turned their attention to building a

These interferometers, located about 250 miles from Los Angeles, were built as part of the U.S. Navy's radio astronomy program. The twin dishes are being used to track and identify radio sources in space.

wider "base" or "receiver" for such a telescope by building several small, steerable dishes, locating them at a distance from one another, and then synchronizing the incoming signals much as our two eyes, set apart, synchronize two separate visual images into one. Four small radio receivers set at the four corners of a football field and so synchronized could act, in effect, the same as a single receiving dish 100 yards (90 m) across in separating fine details in signals.

Such radio telescopes are called *interferometers.* If they are set far enough apart and synchronized for signal receiving, their *resolving power*—we might say their ability to "see," or separate out, fine detail—can be much superior to any single dish, no matter how big. They can receive much more detailed and usable data about more-distant radio sources in the sky. One such array of four synchronized radio telescopes was built at Cambridge University in England in the early 1960s— the first so-called "long-based radio telescope," or "large-array telescope."

Many more such long-based interferometers have since been built. For accuracy, their signals are now synchronized by atomic clocks (modern devices that keep time according to atomic vibrations). Over the years a wide variety of arrays have been used—triangles, circles, or T or Y configurations. One "very-large-array" radio telescope in New Mexico employs more than two dozen separate dishes in a giant Y-shaped array in the desert extending as far as 12 ½ miles (21 km) from one

The Very Large Array (VLA) radio telescope, located near Villa Sororro, New Mexico, is one of the world's most powerful telescopes. Its twenty-seven identical reflector antennas are arranged in a Y-shape, a configuration that allows the VLA to map small, intense radio sources with the highest resolution.

end to the other. This telescope can act as a giant zoom lens to focus sharply on distant galaxies.

From large-array telescopes, it was only a short step to building "very-long-based interferometers." Two telescopes hundreds of miles apart could be synchronized by atomic clocks to provide better information about very distant radio-transmitting galaxies and the mysterious quasars that were just discovered in the 1970s. Then in 1977 an orbitting satellite was used to link and synchronize a radio telescope in West Virginia with one in Ontario, creating, in effect, a receiving "dish" over a thousand miles across! Several such intercontinental linkups now exist, and indeed, there is no technical reason why a radio telescope on Earth could not be linked with one on the Moon to provide an "exceedingly-long-based interferometer."

Finally, we are now beginning to launch both light-gathering telescopes and radio telescopes into space on board orbitting satellites. This will be a major step forward for astronomy. City sky-glow, clouds, and wavering atmospheric currents have long interfered with the full use of Earth-based light-gathering telescopes; and since certain kinds of radio signals are absorbed by Earth's atmosphere and don't reach the surface of the planet, space-based radio telescopes will be a boon to radio astronomers. One satellite-based telescope specially sensitive to infrared radiation is now searching the entire sky for particularly intense heat sources such as those created by newly forming

An artist's conception of a proposed Very Long Baseline Array (VLBA) configuration. The VLBA radio telescope, which will consist of ten large precision antennas distributed from Hawaii to St. Croix, is one of the great technological breakthroughs of modern science and engineering.

stars. Already this search has provided evidence of over a hundred such stars, ranging from very small ones to huge ones, that are forming even now in the Lesser Magellanic Cloud, our second closest neighboring galaxy, confirming that it is a very young, star-forming galaxy.

But radio telescopes have been most useful of all at helping astronomers deal with some of the baffling mysteries of the universe that have only recently come to light—mysteries surrounding such recently discovered wonders as quasars, pulsars, neutron stars, and black holes.

4

THE MYSTERY
OF THE QUASARS

During the 1960s and 70s, as bigger and better radio telescopes were built, a great wave of exploration began. Almost everywhere astronomers turned these telescopes, something new and unsuspected was discovered.

Early on, for example, radar explorations solved some long-standing mysteries about our own Solar System. For centuries, our sister planet Venus had been a baffling enigma to astronomers because of the perpetual layer of thick clouds that concealed its surface from view. No one, for example, had ever been able to determine for sure just how slow or fast Venus turned on its axis, or in which direction it turned, or even if it turned at all! There were no surface markings visible as reference points. But in 1962, by analyzing radar signals reflected back from its rough surface under the cloud layer, radio astronomers proved beyond doubt that Venus did indeed turn on its axis. It turned very slowly compared to Earth's rotation (once every twenty-four hours) completing just one rotation every 243 Earth days. And it turned in the opposite direction from Earth's rotation; on Venus the sun rises in the west and sets in the east!

Three years later the mystery of Mercury's rotation was also solved, once and for all. Astronomers had always thought Mercury turned just once on its axis for every 88-day trip around the sun, with a perpetually hot "bright side" always facing the sun while the other side always faced outer space, perpetually dark and cold. But 1965 radar signals proved that Mercury turned on its axis every 58.7 Earth days, so that all parts of Mercury's surface faced the Sun's broiling heat at some time during every two or three Mercurial years.

MAPPING THE HEAVENS

Important as these "close at home" studies were, far more adventurous projects also got under way. Many early studies involved simply mapping the heavens to see what was there—searching the sky for "radio sources" and then comparing those "hot spots" with star maps made with light telescopes.

The faces of Venus, photographed on nine consecutive days in June 1940

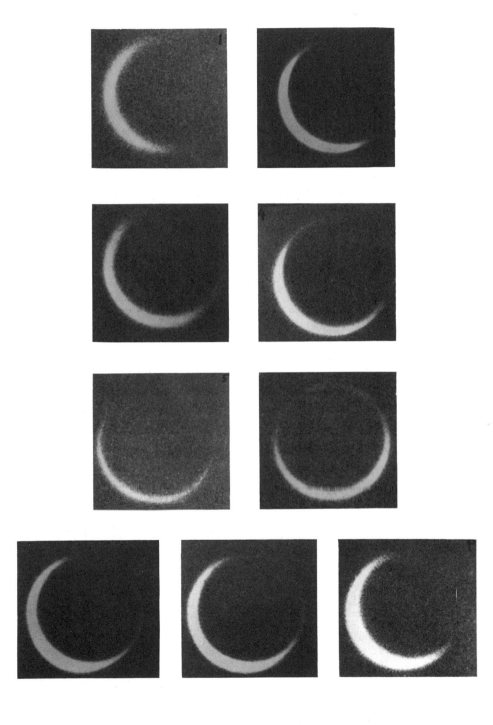

Radio astronomers soon found there was no shortage of radio sources in the sky. Some of these sources did seem to coincide with known light-producing objects—with already-observed colliding galaxies, for example, or with known remnants of *supernova* star explosions in the distant past, events that might be expected to have generated all kinds of radiation. Yet oddly enough, these radio sources seemed to be the exceptions. Many of the brightest stars in the sky turned out to be very feeble radio sources, and for the greatest majority of radio sources, astronomers couldn't find any identifiable light source at all on the star charts.

Many of these radio sources were clearly located in our own Milky Way galaxy, or in other galaxies in the "local cluster" neighboring our own. Bit by bit, radio astronomers were able to build a clearer picture of the nature of these nearby galaxies. The Larger Magellanic Cloud, the nearest galaxy to our own, was believed to be a young galaxy, having formed relatively recently; radio astronomy helped confirm this by discovering, through infrared reception, whole clusters of new, young stars in the process of formation there. In our own galaxy, many areas were unobservable to light telescopes because huge clouds of gas and dust—the stuff new stars are made of—blocked the light. But radio telescopes could pick up some invisible parts of the radio spectrum that could pass right through such gas clouds, helping to develop a clearer picture of what was going on "here at home."

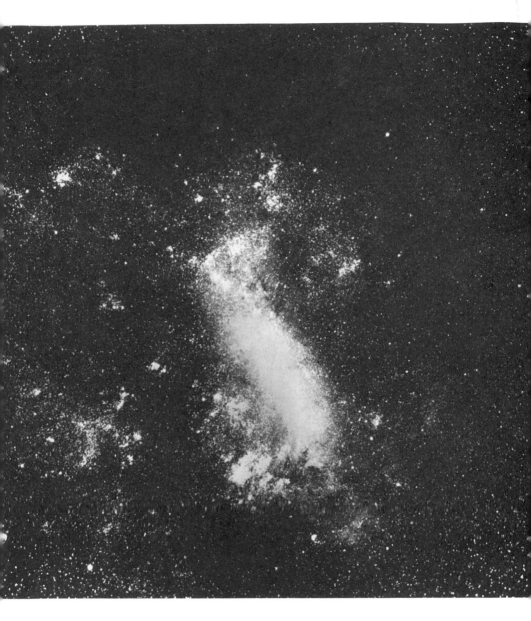

The Larger Magellanic Cloud is the Milky Way's closest galaxy-neighbor

Radio astronomers were just getting their feet on the ground, so to speak, with this kind of exploratory work, when they suddenly encountered a really major challenge—a mystery that no one else had any idea how to deal with.

THE EXPANDING UNIVERSE

In the course of mapping and cataloging radio sources in the sky, one of the things radio astronomers wanted to do was find out where the sources were located, that is, how far away these objects might be from Earth.

Now, determining the distance of stellar objects from Earth is a tricky business. The fact that light and radio waves reach our telescopes from a distant galaxy doesn't tell us how long those signals have been traveling before reaching us, that is, how far away the source of the signal is. But back in the early 1920s, astronomers had found one very useful way to gauge such distances, using a device called a *spectroscope*. This instrument is really just an elaborate version of the prism Newton used to break light up into its colored component wavelengths. Starlight, coming from a distant source and passing through a narrow slit into the spectroscope would be broken up into a series of different-colored bands of light according to wavelength, ranging from violet at one side of the chart to red at the other. These spectral lines, as they are called, showed characteristic colors and patterns according to the atomic composition of the star being observed. One pattern of lines at one place on the spectral band was the "signature" for hydrogen, another pattern indicated helium, another calcium, and so forth. This gave astronomers a great deal of information about the age and other characteristics of the stars they were observing.

But the spectroscope provided another kind of information as well. Astronomers found that the spectral lines of light from an object would shift slightly from their normal place on the spectral scale according to whether the object was moving toward the Earth or away from it. The spectral lines from an object moving toward the Earth would be shifted slightly toward the violet end of the spectrum, while the spectral lines from an object moving away from Earth would be shifted slightly toward the red end of the spectrum. In short, the spectroscope could reveal which direction an object was headed.

This might not seem terribly useful, at first glance, but in fact it proved very important indeed to our understanding of the nature of the universe. In 1921 an astronomer named Edwin Hubble, studying the spectral lines from various stars, made an odd discovery. Although some stars "right here at home" in our own galaxy seemed to be moving toward the Earth while others were moving away, Hubble found that almost every heavenly object outside of our own galaxy seemed to be moving away from us, and the farther away those objects were, the faster they seemed to be moving away. Gradually, astronomers became convinced that this could mean only one thing: the entire universe and everything in it was expanding rapidly. According to this theory, everything in the universe as we know it began this expansion some fifteen billion or more years ago with an enormous explosion, now known to astronomers as the *Big Bang*. All of the stars and galaxies as we see them now, this theory indicates, are the result of that momentous event in the distant past. And the expansion is revealed by the spectral lines of light reaching us from heavenly objects that are still racing away from us—the nearby ones receding slowly and showing just slight red shifts on the spectrograph, more distant ones receding faster and showing more-marked red shifts.

Radio astronomers cataloging radio objects were using this principle to determine roughly how distant a given radio object might be. These spectral lines also provided clues about the nature and composition of these radio objects—whether they were new, just-forming stars, or remnants of supernova explosions, or just energetic gas clouds, or whatnot. Thus one could guess, in general, what each radio object was.

THE QUASI-STELLAR RADIO SOURCES

Then, in 1960, astronomers Allan Sandage and Thomas Matthews, working at the California Institute of Technology, found a radio object that seemed to break all the rules. In the light telescope it appeared to be a small, dim minor star near the edge of our galaxy, never studied carefully because it seemed so totally ordinary. Yet to the radio telescope this "star" appeared to be a veritable beacon of powerful radio signals. Soon three more such humble-appearing "stars" were found, each one actually pouring forth more invisible radio energy than would be expected from whole colliding galaxies!

Puzzled, Sandage and Matthews analyzed the feeble light from these objects with the spectroscope—and the mystery deepened. The spectral lines of these strange "stars" were totally different from those of any known stars in the universe. They were obviously not ordinary stars in any sense, no matter what they looked like. For lack of a better name, these puzzling objects were called "quasi-stellar radio sources." (*Quasi-stellar* means "seeming like, but not actually, a star.") Soon that name was shortened to *quasar*.

Suddenly these radio astronomers found themselves trying to explain celestial objects that were neither stars nor galaxies nor gas clouds nor supernovas nor anything else anyone could think of. What were these strange "radio stars"? And where were they, nearby or distant? As other workers discovered more of these strange objects, another Cal Tech astronomer, Maarten Schmidt, became convinced that the secret to the quasars had to lie in the spectral lines created by their light—the lines that made no sense. Studying the spectral lines from one of these objects, Schmidt found four that seemed to be familiar. These lines looked like the pattern characteristic of hydrogen, but they were located in the wrong part of the spectrum altogether. The hydrogen pattern was normally found toward the blue end of the spectrum, whereas these lines were far to the red side of the spectrum, shifted a full 16 percent out of hydrogen's normal place! This red shift was far greater than any ever measured before for any heavenly object.

If these *were* hydrogen lines (and Schmidt soon confirmed that they were), this had to mean that this dim "star" was one of the most fantastically distant objects ever before discovered, 2 billion light-years away and racing away from our galaxy at an unbelievable 27,000 miles (43,450 km) per second. And if that were the case, this "object," whatever it was, had to be pouring out light and radio energy with a brilliance greater than a hundred galaxies of a hundred billion stars each, all taken together! Soon after, astronomers identified another quasar with an even greater red shift, placing it more than 4 billion light-years away and receding from us faster than 50,000 miles (80,500 km) per second.

WHAT ARE THEY?

Within a few years, several hundred more quasars were identified. All were apparently at staggering distances, near the outer fringes of the known universe. All were emitting stupendous amounts of radio energy, and all were racing away from us at incredible speeds. At least two quasars appeared so distant that they were recedinging from our galaxy at some 80 percent of the speed of light.

Slowly astronomers gathered data about these mysterious objects, but for every answer they found there were new and baffling questions. At first it was thought that these objects might not really be so far distant after all, that maybe something else accounted for the giant red shifts. Some astronomers argued that they might be relatively nearby objects that were rushing away from us for some simple, local reason—perhaps hurled away from the heart of a nearby galaxy by some kind of colossal explosion. But where was other evidence of such an explosion? Other researchers found that individual, separate radio sources *within* quasars seemed to be moving apart at several times the speed of light, which is considered impossible according to the principles of modern physics. Only if quasars were really much closer would the movement of these radio sources calculate out to a speed safely below light speed. But this explanation didn't seem to fit, either. As time passed, more and more evidence indicated that quasars really *were* as distant as they seemed to be, pouring out their incredible radiation.

Even more baffling, many of the quasars were found to vary greatly in the amount of light and energy they released over periods of time, growing brighter and dimmer and brighter again in a matter of hours, days, or weeks. This seemed to suggest that whatever they were, they weren't very stable. It also suggested that they weren't really very large, not nearly as large, for example, as an ordinary garden-variety galaxy like our own. In fact, it seemed possible that the center of a quasar from which all the energy was pouring might not be much bigger than an ordinary star!

So where was all that energy coming from in such a relatively small celestial object? Nobody could say, for sure. But at the same time radio astronomers were puzzling over the mystery of the quasars, they were making other discoveries that would provide clues to the mystery. These discoveries had to do with certain previously unsuspected heavenly objects known today as *pulsars, neutron stars,* and *black holes.*

5

PULSARS
AND NEUTRON STARS

For a number of years, radio astronomers were at an impasse trying to explain what the mysterious quasars might actually be. As these strange objects were studied, certain characteristics of the quasars became increasingly clear—and they just didn't make sense. All of them were almost certainly extremely distant, far out toward the edge of the observable universe, and racing away from our part of the universe at staggering speeds. Each one of them was radiating incredible amounts of light and other electromagnetic waves—more than a hundred times the amount of radiation poured out by an ordinary galaxy like our Milky Way.

But if they *were* immense galaxies, they ought to have appeared as oval smudges like other galaxies, even at their great distances—and they didn't. Instead, they appeared as starlike pinpoints, even in our largest telescopes. Many also appeared to be unstable, with large variations in their radiation over months or years, a fact that led astronomers to believe they must really be quite small. And finally astronomers knew of no kind of celestial object that could radiate such fantastic amounts of energy for very long; some researchers calculated that with this kind of energy-outpouring, quasars might only last for a million years or so before "burning out." This notion was supported by the discovery by astronomer Allen Sandage in 1965 of some blue starlike objects equally distant as quasars, and still pouring out visible light, but without the radio emissions. These so-called "blue stellar objects," or BSOs, were thought to be aging or dying quasars.

All these characteristics of quasars became familiar to astronomers, but they still did not solve the mystery of what the quasars are and how they got where they are. This had to wait upon some other radio-astronomy discoveries.

THE FLICKERING PULSARS

As it happened, quasars were not the only odd things radio astronomers were turning up during the 1960s and 70s. Some other seemingly inexplicable objects were also appearing in their radio telescopes.

One such thing caught the attention of astronomers at the Mullard Radio Astronomy Laboratory in Cambridge, England, in 1967: a radio object with an intermittent signal. Unlike other radio objects in our own galaxy, which emitted steady, constant signals, this object seemed to pulsate, sending out a sharp burst of radio signals every 1.3 seconds, like clockwork. Soon other such pulsating radio objects were discovered, some also visible in light telescopes, some not.

These objects were definitely not quasars. For one thing, all of them were in our own Milky Way galaxy, and the changes in radiation were not the slow waxing and waning characteristic of quasars. These objects all seemed to pulsate at very short intervals, ranging from as little as 1/300 of a second to as long as 4 seconds—but no longer. By the early 1980s some three hundred of these objects, now spoken of as *pulsars,* had been cataloged. One of them actually pulsates once every 1/1,000 of a second. Astronomers call it "the millisecond pulsar."

But what were they? They definitely were not the ordinary *variable stars* that astronomers had known about for many years. Long before radio telescopes had come along, astronomers using light telescopes had found that many stars in our galaxy grow brighter and dimmer over regular periods of time, ranging from a matter of a few hours at one extreme to several years at the other. There are a number of possible reasons why such stars might vary in luminosity in this fashion. It is known, for example, that many of these variable stars are so-called *eclipsing binaries.* These are double stars—often one small, bright star and one large, dim one—which revolve in orbit around each other. When the plane of their orbits is in our line of sight, the large dim star will pass in front of

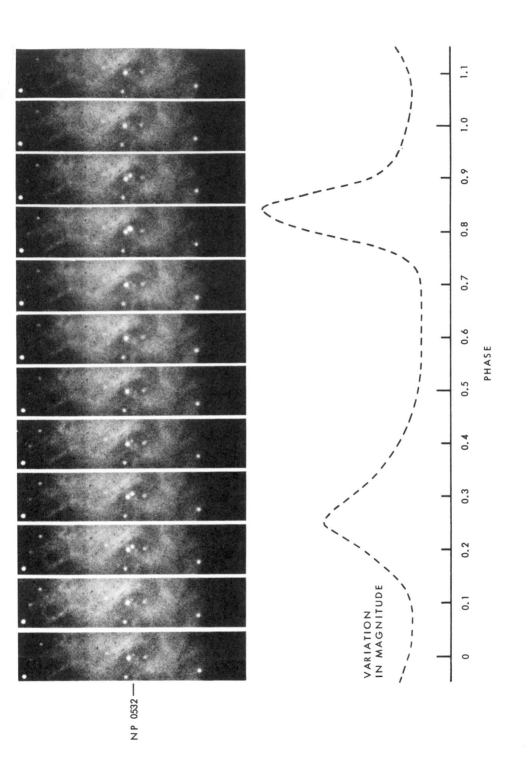

N P 0532

VARIATION
IN MAGNITUDE

PHASE

0   0.1   0.2   0.3   0.4   0.5   0.6   0.7   0.8   0.9   1.0   1.1

the smaller brighter one with each revolution, eclipsing it and obscuring the light from the bright one on a regular basis. This is what happens to the star known as Algol, which is eclipsed by its larger companion every 2.87 days. During each such eclipse the light from Algol becomes three times dimmer than normal until the eclipse is over.

In other variable stars, their light changes result from something going on in the star itself. Some are known to be either large, newly forming stars or old, dying stars with such unstable nuclear reactions going on at their cores and on their surfaces that the light they emit will brighten or dim at intervals. Many thousands of such stars are known—so many, in fact, that astronomers find it a time-consuming nuisance to try to keep track of them all and chart their variations, scientifically important as that may be. To help with this problem, there is an organization known as the American Association of Variable Star Observers, founded in 1911. Its eleven hundred members include many amateurs around the world who have shouldered the major responsibility for monitoring these variables.

Another group of variable stars, called Cepheids, are supergiant stars which are known to be

A sequence and graph showing pulsations of a pulsar within the debris of the Crab Nebula

alternately expanding and contracting at rates that range from 1 to 100 days. For years astronomers have found the Cepheid variables to be an important tool for determining the size of our galaxy and measuring the distance to other galaxies.

But none of these variable stars had ever shown the rapid-fire pulsation of the newly discovered pulsars. How could any star in a binary system revolve around its neighbor once every 1/300 of a second? How could any changing nuclear reactions produce such a rapidly pulsating phenomenon? Clearly the pulsars had to be some kind of heavenly body other than any of the known stars.

Like all scientists before them faced with a mystery, radio astronomers had to start with what they could actually observe and then try to imagine what might be causing what they observed. There was no question that the pulsars were producing extremely rapid bursts of radio signals—it was as if they were tops spinning rapidly in the sky emitting bursts of radio waves with every revolution. And indeed, astronomers soon became convinced that the pulsars had to be spinning very rapidly to do what they were doing. But any object the size of a star would simply be torn apart by such rapid rotation. This meant that a pulsar could not be any ordinary kind of star. For one thing, it would have to be extremely small—maybe only a few *miles* in diameter—and extremely dense, with a powerful gravity. And, of course, there had to be some reason for it to emit enormous bursts of radio signals.

NEUTRON STARS

One kind of object astronomers knew about that more or less fit this picture was a *white dwarf* star, the dimming cinder of a dying star which has burnt out and collapsed in on itself after most of its nuclear fuels have been exhausted. But even a white dwarf would be far too large, with far too little gravity, to hold together if it rotated as fast as a pulsar had to be rotating. A pulsar couldn't be a white dwarf, but it would have to be something like a white dwarf.

Today, astronomers believe that pulsars are indeed like white dwarfs in certain ways, only more so. They are the end results of enormous supernova star explosions. This kind of cataclysmic event occurs when a huge, supermassive star collapses in on itself. This causes a stupendous release of atomic energy in a staggering explosion which hurls the major portion of the star in the form of gas and dust in all directions into space. What remains of the star collapses into itself under an immense force of gravity. Matter in the small core of the star is incredibly compressed. Electrons and protons of the atoms are smashed together to form neutrons, and those neutrons, without any electric charge, are crushed down together, tighter and tighter. This packing of neutrons under intense gravitational pressure creates a *neutron star*— intensely hot, intensely dense, but very tiny. A neutron star might actually have twice the mass of our own sun, yet only be some 12 miles (20 km) in

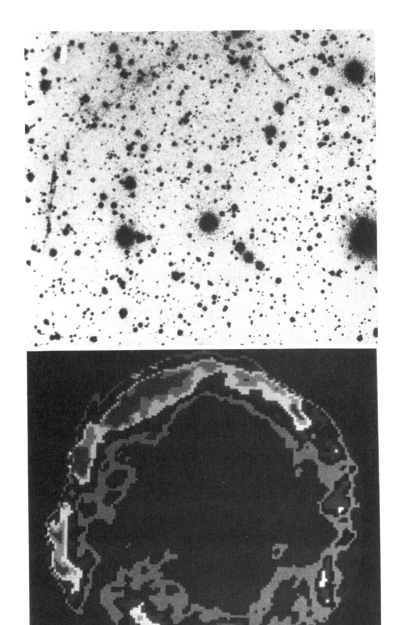

diameter, and be so dense that a single teaspoonful of its material would weigh billions of tons!

What's more, a neutron star can spin on its axis very rapidly indeed without breaking apart, because of its incredibly concentrated gravity—certainly as rapidly as the fast-spinning pulsars, or even faster. Astronomers also calculated that a neutron star might also have a very intense magnetic field, and that electrons swirling past its magnetic poles could generate veritable beacons of radio waves. Thus, if the magnetic pole of a neutron star should happen to swing in the Earth's direction with every rotation, a burst of radio waves would strike our radio telescopes with every rotation, like a rotating lighthouse-beam of light—exactly what we knew was happening with pulsars! As more and more evidence poured in, it became increasingly evident that pulsars *are* rapidly rotating neutron stars, the dying remnants of supernova star explosions, nothing more nor less.

One final bit of evidence has helped confirm this theory of pulsars. With the vast amount of electromagnetic energy being emitted—and thus lost—by a neutron star, astronomers calculated

Tycho's Supernova Remnant
Top: Optical image (Palomar Observatory). Bottom: Radio image (The National Radio Astronomy Observatory)

that over the years the rapid rotation of such a star would have to begin to slow down ever so slightly. This idea was tested in the case of a pulsar found in the center of the Crab Nebula, the remnants of a supernova explosion known to have become visible to us nine hundred years ago. The neutron star–pulsar formed in that explosion is now believed to have been rotating on its axis 1,000 times a second in the beginning. But when discovered by our radio telescopes in the 1960s, it was rotating only 30 times a second. Careful radio-telescope studies done in the early 1970s showed that the radio pulses from the Crab-Nebula pulsar actually *were* slowing down by some 36 billionths of a second each day—not very much, but slowing down just the same. After another twelve hundred years, its rotation will only be 15 times per second instead of 30.

The discovery of pulsars, and their final identification as neutron stars, was a great triumph for radio astronomy. But these discoveries had another value as well. They provided a major clue to help solve the unsolved mystery of the quasars.

6

GRAVITATIONAL COLLAPSE AND BLACK HOLES

Neutron stars were fascinating objects to astronomers and astrophysicists. Containing nothing but crushed-together atoms stripped down to neutrons, they represented a state of matter nobody had ever thought of before. They were extremely small, extremely dense, with almost unbelievably powerful gravitational fields. Indeed, their gravity was so extreme that nothing except speeding electrons, light, and electromagnetic waves could escape from their gravitational pull. Yet these stars were nothing but the dying, burned-out remnants of colossal star explosions. Very soon on the cosmic time scale a neutron star–pulsar would slow down its rotation, lose all of its electrons, cease to pulsate, and cool down to the bitter cold of outer space, a lightless dead cinder—the final bitter end of life for one kind of star.

THE CONCEPT OF
GRAVITATIONAL
COLLAPSE

But suppose there were a super-
nova type of explosion that involved some struc-
ture far bigger than the kind that produces a
neutron star? Suppose a still more enormous and
much heavier star exploded as a supernova? Physicists calculated that such a supernova explosion of
just one very huge, massive star might result in a
collapse of matter toward the center so great, with
such intense pressure of gravity, that even the
tightly packed neutrons of a neutron star would be
smashed together and broken up—literally crushed
out of existence! Under ever-increasing pressure of
gravity, the matter of the star would be squashed
down to the diameter of a planet like Earth, then
to the diameter of a volley ball, then down to a
dimensionless point in space—what physicists
would call a *singularity*—and finally disappear
altogether. In such a process, the force of gravity at
the center would become so intense that nothing
could escape to the outside, not even light or radio
waves. The result, in theory, would be a *black hole*
in space, growing smaller and smaller, its gravita-
tion rising higher and higher, so that all the matter
anywhere in its near vicinity would be sucked into
it and just disappear.

At first this concept of gravitational collapse
leading to a black hole seemed little more than a

mathematical exercise. You could show that it should happen, but you couldn't prove it ever did. Obviously nobody could see such a black hole in space directly by any instruments astronomers have available. There couldn't be any light or radio waves coming from it—it would just be a spot of "emptiness" in empty space. So how could you ever prove any such thing actually existed, or detect one if it were there?

Radio astronomers found a way. First, they assumed that a black hole would have to be formed if the right conditions of a supercolossal explosion occurred. Mathematics said so. And since such conditions must have occurred at one time or another, they assumed that black holes were out there; you just couldn't see them or detect them readily. Finally, they calculated that if there were anything—a nearby star, for instance—in the near vicinity of a black hole, material from that star would be constantly swirling into the black hole, and that such violently agitated material should emit X rays that our radio telescopes could detect.

In 1971 just such an object was found. An X-ray-detecting telescope carried on a satellite found a strong X-ray source in the constellation Cygnus. The source was very near a huge blue star. That star was a binary, one star in a two-star system. Its companion star couldn't be seen at all, but it seemed to be an intense source of the X rays. Astronomers believe that the invisible "companion star" is in fact an actual black hole, sucking matter away from the visible star and generating X rays in the process. And if one such black hole exists, many more must exist also.

Here at last was a possible clue to the mystery of the quasars, with their enormous outpourings of light and energy from the outer edges of our universe. From the first, astronomers had realized that these galaxy-size objects had to be undergoing some kind of colossal explosive events in their interiors—the collision of stars in the midst of galaxies, for example, or the occurrence of supernova explosions in their central portions. As their understanding of pulsars, neutron stars, and black holes has developed, most astronomers now believe that massive explosions in the midst of quasar-galaxies have caused giant black holes to form in their centers, with the huge amounts of matter falling into them generating powerful beacons of X rays. These black holes might have the mass of a whole galaxy concentrated and pressed down into a volume smaller than a neutron star. And this idea that a black hole lies at the core of every quasar is borne out by the fact that so many of the known quasars are X-ray emitters. In fact, some astronomers think that almost all of the X-ray radiation reaching our radio telescopes comes from quasars with black holes at the center.

The constellation Cygnus

THE RADIO TIME MACHINE

So it is that astronomers are now reasonably confident they know what quasars are, thanks to radio astronomy. But there are still many fascinating unanswered questions about these remarkable objects. We may know *what* they are (or were), but *when* were they? What are they *now*? Why are they all so far away, with none at all in the closer parts of the universe? Most of them are 10 to 12 billion light-years away (although a very few have been placed somewhat closer, at only about 3 to 4 billion light-years away).

Think for a minute what we mean when we speak of receiving radio waves and light from quasars 10 to 12 billion light-years away. A *light-year* is the distance that light can travel (at the speed of light, of course) in a year's time. We know that anything we see in the sky with a telescope merely represents what was happening when the light or signal left the source. It takes light over eight minutes, for example, to travel from our own Sun to Earth. This means that when you glance at the Sun, what you are seeing is actually what was happening there more than eight minutes ago. When you look at Alpha Centauri in a telescope, what you are seeing actually happened over four years ago, because it has taken the light you are seeing now more than four years to reach Earth from that nearest neighboring star. Although it's not likely, Alpha Centauri could actually have had a nova explosion more than two years ago, and we

The two stars dominating this photo,
Alpha *and* Beta Centauri, *are*
the closest known stars to the Sun.

wouldn't know it for another two years. In a sense, when you look through a telescope at Alpha Centauri, you are looking through a telescopic time machine, observing something that happened sometime in the past. And the farther away the light-emitting or radio-wave-emitting object, the farther into the past you are looking.

By the same token, when radio astronomers first identified quasars from radio waves and X-ray emissions and found that those quasars were 10 to 12 billion light-years away, this meant that what they were observing were actually events going on ten to twelve billion years ago, not today. And since we know those quasars have been moving away from us faster and faster for that whole ten to twelve billion years, what astronomers are observing now must have been happening *much closer* to us than the quasars are now. And since astronomers now believe that the original "Big Bang" that started our known universe forming and expanding occurred only some fifteen-or-so billion years ago, this must mean that what we are now observing going on in the quasars must actually have been something going on quite early in the formation of the universe, when conditions were much different than they are now. Possibly one reason that almost all quasars are so far away (and so long ago) and the reason we don't see any that are closer (and thus more recent) is that the kind of catastrophic events in the universe's early stages that caused the quasars to form in the long-distant past simply aren't happening anymore, and, in fact, haven't been happening for several billion years.

If what we observe of quasars today is actually observing what was happening with them ten to twelve billion years ago, then what are those same quasars actually doing now—today? Of course, no one knows, but there are some clues. Astronomers know that radio-emitting neutron stars and pulsars are *evolving*—slowing down and changing. The life of a neutron star until it finally becomes a cold, dead cinder may be only about four billion years. Astronomers speculate that black holes also evolve and change. Perhaps in a few billion years they ultimately contract down into a tiny, dense black spot the size of a walnut, or a pinpoint, or even smaller, no longer emitting X rays or anything else, and then finally vanish to all intents and purposes. Some astronomers think black holes may ultimately simply disappear, leaving no trace behind.

If things of this sort happen to a quasar in the course of, say, four or five billion years, then many of the quasars astronomers have identified may not even exist anymore. And others, racing away from us faster and faster, at up to 80 percent the speed of light *when the light we are now receiving left them*, may long since have *passed* the speed of light relative to us, so that no light or radio signal can any longer ever reach us. As far as observing them further is concerned, they *have* disappeared, moving forever beyond the edge of the universe observable to us, into perpetual darkness.

Of course ten years from now—or five—or one, we may see things entirely differently. It was just over fifty years ago that a chance discovery of a radio engineer provided us with an incredibly powerful and previously unthought-of astronomical tool—the radio telescope. During the course of that time, radio astronomers with better and better instruments and greater and greater understanding have made some of the most major discoveries in all the history of astronomy. They still have far to go in explaining where the universe came from, how it is constructed, how it got that way, and what will happen to it next. And surely there is no reason to imagine that all the major discoveries about the universe have already been made. The work of radio astronomy is indeed a never-ending quest. We can be sure the next fifty years will be just as exciting as the last.

GLOSSARY

"Big Bang"—A theory, widely accepted by scientists, that the universe as we know it and everything in it began some 15 to 20 billion years ago with an enormous explosion. According to this theory, the universe has been expanding steadily ever since.

Black hole—an area at the core of a burnt-out, collapsing star where gravitational pressure has become so great that no radiation, not even light, can escape. All that can be detected is a small area of "emptiness."

Cosmic rays—high energy radiation and sub-atomic particles which originate in outer space and strike the earth with great penetrating power.

Eclipsing binaries—double stars (often a large, dim star and a smaller bright one) that move in orbit around each other so that the dim star regularly *eclipses* or moves in front of the bright one, dimming its light. One form of "variable star."

Electromagnetic spectrum—a broad band or *spectrum* of radiation of varying wavelength, including visible light, ultraviolet and infrared light, microwaves, radio waves, X rays, gamma rays and cosmic rays.

Focus—a point in front of the reflecting mirror of a reflector telescope where reflected light waves come together to form a sharp image. The curve of the mirror causes the light waves to focus in this fashion.

Gamma rays—high-energy rays emitted from the nuclei of some radioactive atoms as they decay to lower energy levels.

Infrared waves—essentially invisible *heat* radiation which lies just below the band of visible red light in the spectrum.

Interferometer—a type of radio telescope with two or more receiving dishes set apart from each other, with incoming signals synchronized to provide more detailed, usable data than single-receiver telescopes can provide. Sometimes called *large-array telescopes*.

Light-year—a measure of distance based on the amount that light travels at 186,000 miles per second for a whole year, or about 5.8 *trillion* miles. The nearest star to our sun is about 3.5 light-years away.

Microwaves—high-energy waves with wavelengths longer than visible light but shorter than radio waves. These are the waves that cook food in a microwave oven.

Neutron star—the collapsing, exceedingly dense core of a burned-out star, in which the atoms have been crushed down into neutrons. Many neutron stars spin very rapidly on their axes and emit pulselike bursts of radiation at very brief intervals. See also *pulsar.*

Parabola—the special curve, slightly deeper than circular, used for the reflecting mirror of a reflector telescope. A mirror with this curve focuses all light waves that strike it to a single focal point.

Prism—a block of glass or quartz, often triangular in shape, which will break up white sunlight into its colored-light components in a rainbow spectrum or band.

Pulsar—a rapidly spinning neutron star so oriented in space that it emits rapid pulses of radiation detectable by our radio telescopes. See also *neutron star.*

Quasar—a "quasi-stellar radio source"—that is, a celestial object that looks like a star, but pours out far greater quantities of radiation. Most astronomers now believe that quasars are distant galaxies in which super-explosions have caused giant black holes to form. Their powerful beacons of X rays and other radiation are fed by surrounding matter being sucked into the intense gravitational fields of the black holes.

"Quasi-stellar"—seeming like, but not actually, a star. The term "quasi-stellar radio source," first applied to a celestial object discovered in 1960, was soon replaced by "quasar."

Radar—comes from *RA*dio *D*etecting *A*nd *R*anging. A system for detecting and locating objects by bouncing radio waves off them and measuring the time it takes for the reflected beam to return.

Radio astronomy—a branch of astronomy in which instruments (i.e., *radio telescopes*) capable of detecting invisible radiation are used to study celestial objects.

Radio waves—electromagnetic waves of medium to long wavelength which can be used to transmit radio, television, and wireless telephone messages.

Reflector telescope—a telescope in which a parabolic mirror in one end of a tube gathers light from a celestial object and reflects it to form a sharp image at a point of focus. A magnifying lens at the point of focus then enlarges the image for clear visual observation.

Refractor telescope—a telescope with lenses at either end of a tube. Light from a celestial object is gathered by a large lens and *refracted* or bent down the tube to focus on a smaller magnifying lens where an enlarged image of the object can be observed.

Resolving power—the power of any telescope to produce a clear, sharp, detailed image of the object under study (or sharp, detailed information about that object). In general, the greater its resolving power, the more useful the telescope for studying the universe.

Singularity—to astronomers, a single point in space that may contain an enormous amount of matter, but has no dimensions at all. Some scientists think that a black hole, with all of its matter crushed tighter and tighter together under an ever-increasing force of gravity, eventually becomes a singularity.

Spectroscope—an elaborate version of the prism Newton used to break up light into its colored components. Starlight passing through a narrow slit in the spectroscope is broken up into different colored bands of light of different wavelengths. Characteristic colors and patterns reveal the atomic composition of the star being observed.

Spectrum—a continuous band or array of light waves or other waves arranged in the order of increasing wave lengths. The *light spectrum* contains the rainbow band of various-colored visible light. The *electromagnetic spectrum* includes the light spectrum as well as other waves of shorter or longer wavelengths.

Supernova—an explosion of a large dying star in which most of its matter is blown away in the form of gases and dust in all directions, leaving behind a neutron star or pulsar.

Variable star—a star which grows dimmer and brighter in a regular, predictable sequence. Some variable stars are *eclipsing binaries*. Others grow brighter and dimmer because of periodic changes in the sub-atomic reactions on the star's surface or at its center.

White dwarf—the burnt-out glowing cinder of a star which has exhausted its nuclear fuel and has collapsed on itself. The matter making up a white dwarf is packed tight and extremely dense.

X rays—a form of electromagnetic radiation, similar to light but of much shorter wavelength, capable of penetrating objects such as the human body. In an X-ray machine, X rays are generated when a metal target in a cathode ray tube is bombarded by a stream of electrons. X rays are also generated during celestial explosions.

ADDITIONAL READING

Asimov, Isaac. *Asimov's Biographical Encyclopedia of Science and Technology.* 2d rev. ed. New York: Doubleday, 1982.

———. *Asimov's Guide to Science.* New York: Basic Books, 1972. Pp. 20–94.

Baugher, Joseph F. *The Space Age Solar System.* New York: John Wiley & Sons, 1988.

Considine, D.M., ed. *Van Nostrand's Scientific Encyclopedia.* 6th ed. New York: Van Nostrand Reinhold, 1983.

Hartmann, W.K., and Miller, R. *Cycles of Fire.* New York. Workman Publishing, 1987.

Hoyle, Fred. *Galaxies, Nuclei and Quasars.* New York: Harper & Row, 1965.

Nourse, Alan E. *Universe, Earth and Atom: The Story of Physics.* New York: Harper & Row, 1969. Pp. 389–458.

"The Once and Future Universe." *National Geographic,* vol. 163, no. 6, June 1983. Pp. 704–749.

INDEX

Radio telescopes (*continued*)
  intercontinental linkups,
    51
  Jodrell Bank, 40, *41*, 42
  large-array, 47, *48*, 49, *50*,
    51, *52*
  resolution, 44
  uses and techniques, 42,
    44
Radio waves, 35, 39
  discovery of, 9, *10*, 11
Reber, Grote, 11–13, *14*, 15,
  17, 39, 40
Red shifts, 62, 64, 65
Reflection of light, 27, *28*
Reflector telescopes, 27, *28*, 31
Refraction of light, 27, *28*, 31
Refractor telescopes, 27, *28*
Resolution, 44
Resolving power, 49
Rotation of planets, 55–56

Sagan, Carl, 46
Sagittarious (constellation), 11
Sandage, Allan, 62, 63, 68
Satellite-based telescopes, 51,
  79
Satellites, radio telescope
  tracking of, 40, *41*
Saturn, radar mapping of, 42
Schmidt, Maarten, 63, 64
Search for Extraterrestrial In-
  telligence (SETI), 46–47
Singularity, 78
Solar system, 29, 55–56
  history of study, 19–27
  See also specific planets
Soviet Union, 27, 40
Spectral lines, 60–64
Spectroscopes, 60, 61, 63
Speed of light, 24, 26, 34, 65,
  85
Sputnik I, 40
Stars:
  distance from Earth, 60–
    62

formation of, 51, 53, 58,
  62, 71, 73
supernova explosions, 15,
  58, 62, 73, *74*, 75, 77,
  78, 79, 80, 82
variable, 69, 71–72
Sun, 10, 23, 29, 46, 56, 82, 83
  as source of radio radia-
    tion, 15
Sunspots, 23
Supernova explosions, 15, 58,
  62, 73, *74*, 75, 77, 78, 79,
  80, 82

Telescopes, 35, 56, 69
  history of, 23, *24–25*, 26–
    31
  radio, *see* Radio telescopes,
  satellite-based, 51, 79
Tycho's supernova remnant, *74*

Ultraviolet light, 31, 33, *34*
Universe, expansion of, 60–62,
  84

Variable stars, 69, 71–72
Venus, 55–56, *57*
  radar mapping of, 42, *45*
Very Large Array (VLA) radio
  telescope, 49, *50*, 51
Very Long Baseline Array
  (VLBA) radio telescope, 51,
  52
Visible light waves, 19, 33, *34*,
  35, *36*

Wavelengths of light, 31–37,
  60
White dwarf star, 73
White light, *36*
World War II, 39, 40

X rays, 35, 79–80

Zodiacal constellations, *20*